Hi, friend.

My name is Big.

I have a big problem.

BUNNY
WILL NOT
BE QUIET!

WRITTEN AND ILLUSTRATED
BY JASON THARP

Ready-to-Read

Simon Spotlight
New York   London   Toronto   Sydney   New Delhi

When you want to do something big—
DON'T BE QUIET! Sharing your dreams
with others will help you get there.
I believe in you.

SIMON SPOTLIGHT
An imprint of Simon & Schuster Children's Publishing Division
1230 Avenue of the Americas, New York, New York 10020
This Simon Spotlight edition May 2020
Copyright © 2020 by Jason Tharp
SIMON SPOTLIGHT, READY-TO-READ, and colophon are registered trademarks of Simon & Schuster, Inc.
For information about special discounts for bulk purchases, please contact Simon & Schuster Special Sales
at 1-866-506-1949 or business@simonandschuster.com.
Manufactured in the United States of America 0320 LAK
10 9 8 7 6 5 4 3 2 1
This book has been cataloged with the Library of Congress.
ISBN 978-1-5344-6638-8 (hc)
ISBN 978-1-5344-6637-1 (pbk)
ISBN 978-1-5344-6639-5 (eBook)

He yells at plays.